NATURE'S NOMADS

MAJ GEN KRISHAN CHAUHAN

Creative CROWS
PUBLISHERS LLP

Published by

Creative CROWS PUBLISHERS LLP
the publishing & communication people

Office: A-42, Dayanand Colony,

New Delhi(South)-110024

Emails: ganivpanjrath@yahoo.co.in, tannaazirani@gmail.com

ISBN-13: 978-93-91526-19-1

ISBN 10: 93-91526-19-5

MRP: Rs. 299/-

Book size: 5*8

DEDICATION

I dedicate this book to the amazing animal and tree life of this vast country. Our snow-covered mountains, deserts, huge water bodies as well forests have hundreds of thousands of these Godly creations.

I have had the opportunity to live in various regions of this country during the last seventy years, thanks to frequent postings of my father in my youth and later when I served as an officer of the Indian Army.

I thank the Indian Army for the experiences it gave me, which I could use to write stories on such diverse topics.

PREFACE

Mother Nature is worshipped as Prakriti Mata in India; because she has bestowed upon us wonderful flora and fauna. All species, knowingly or unknowingly, help others and Mother Earth in its regrowth. Species are usually confined to separate regions, but there are certain exceptions. Migratory birds are well known for long distance travels. Some species have been brought by humans to newer continents while others have accidentally boarded ships or aircraft and have established new homes in new places. It is interesting to have a peek in the life of such nomads.

If only they could speak!

There are certain creatures whom we fear, hate; and then there are a few that fill humans with loathing. An effort has been made in this book to understand them by weaving stories around their lifestyle.

Another subject broached upon is that of the nomadic street children. Often in dirty, torn clothes, these hungry children may be seen as beggars, ragpickers or petty thieves. However, if given a chance their inherent resilience helps them to achieve their true potential. The Reader, after going through the stories in this book, may view these vagabonds and nomads in a different light.

ACKNOWLEDGEMENT

The idea for such an unusual book originated while researching an article for my blog on WordPress, on how trees communicate and help each other. If trees could communicate, then animals could speak too!

I thank my wife, Reeta for sharing her views on this interesting subject. She has been very patient and helpful in the past one year during which the book was written. She has helped me immensely in typing and sending the manuscript and its amendments to the publishers. I am grateful to her. My daughters, Jyotsna and Anisha kept my motivation level high. They also helped me with the photographs. My grandchildren, Aryan, Netanya, Amaira and Ira read my stories and provided valuable inputs. I acknowledge their support.

I am indebted to Ganiv Panjrath and Tannaaz Irani my publishers at Creative Crows Publishers and their team. They had nurtured me as an author during my first book. In the second book too, their help is immense. I am especially thankful to Tannaaz who has edited my stories paragraph by paragraph. She has a special aptitude to convert some complex portions of the stories into easily understandable prose.

CONTENTS

1

THE RED GHOSTS OF TALSARI BEACH

CHRISTMAS ISLAND

In the Indian Ocean, between Australia and Java, is a tiny island called Christmas Island. In the Hosnies Spring area of this island, Rudy and Cindy lived in their respective underground homes. Like the millions of other red crabs, they had their own burrows of sand and pebbles, the entrances covered carefully with leaves and twigs. They needed to live in an area that had higher humidity as they breathed through their gills. For this reason, they came out of their dwellings only in the early morning. They ate dead leaves, fruits and seedlings and once in a while, dead insects too. Thus, they were part of nature's scavengers who kept the drier part of the mangrove clean. Having had their fill, they returned home before it grew too hot. In the summer they hibernated for most of the time.

For three years Rudy had been eyeing Cindy. Now they were mature and hence ready for the beach lunar festival. The mature male crabs left all their homes almost simultaneously, in a very large group. Oh, what a sight! A red carpet moving among the greens of the forest till they reached the road.

Here, the humans, who acted as caretakers, had a guide in place. He guided them to an over-bridge for crossing the road. Until just a few years ago, thousands of the red crabs would regularly come under the monstrous black tyres of moving vehicles. Most died; others were left severely injured.

The march continued on the other side of the road. Another danger was lurking on their route ahead. An army of Crazy Yellow ants attacked their flanks. Hundreds of them would pounce on a single crab, at first blinding it, then biting it in the abdomen till it opened out; and then they would feast on its guts. One by one, the dying crabs of the flanks were carried away by the hungry ants. Rudy was glad he wasn't in the flanks else he would be dead by now. The rest kept marching till they all reached the beach.

Rudy was happy to be at the beach. He found himself an excellent location where water would not reach him during high tide. Then he went on to make a bigger burrow…a burrow for Cindy and himself. A burrow so good, that Cindy would find it irresistible. In a week's time, Cindy would come with other females. He prayed for her, that she would not get killed by the Crazy Yellow ants. He prayed that she would find him from amongst the hundreds of thousands of red crabs.

Finally, it was festival day. The females came in droves and were welcomed by the males. It was a time for merry making, dance and romance. But Rudy had his eyes peeled only for Cindy. He looked around for her anxiously and was relieved when he found her. Cindy was a little shy and unsure. But once he showed her his burrow, she agreed to be his mate. The merriment continued until late into the night. After a week, one morning, it was time for Rudy to go home, back to the mangrove. Cindy stayed in the beach side burrow for a few days. Then one night, in the last quarter of the moon, she laid the eggs for a new brood. She carried them over her back into the sea. Then she went back, towards the mangrove.

THE INDIAN OCEAN

The tide carried millions of eggs of these red crabs' into the ocean. They turned into larvae. Looking like shrimps, the larvae called megalopae were great swimmers. They were food to many fishes too; till they matured into tiny little red crabs. Most of them returned to the beach and on to their mangrove in Hosnies Spring where they would finally settle like their parents. Rudy Junior, Cindy Junior, Dicky and Chloe allowed themselves to be swept into the deeper part of the ocean. Some instinct told them that Christmas Island was not safe for them because of the Crazy Yellow ants. But they had no inkling of how many days it might take them to reach another, suitable land mass. These adventurous friends did not know what dangers lay ahead. A colony of jellyfish awaited their arrival. They thought these red crabs were easy meat for them if they ventured too close. They even charmed the quartet with their graceful movements. Cindy fell into their trap and went ahead. At the last moment, Rudy Junior swam faster than Cindy and forced her to change directions. It was a close call, no doubt. Night was spent huddled together with one of them on guard against sharks and eels.

As they entered Bay of Bengal, their scout, Dicky spotted a school of large striped bass fish. He told his friends to sink down as much as possible and allow the school to pass, without eyeing them. There were many such close shaves in their incredible journey of four thousand kilometres, but the four of them managed to hit the Talsari beach of Orissa, India. A fine morning and a golden beach; perfect they thought, as they walked on the beach. Nevertheless, they had to go to a nearby mangrove for at least three years. Only then they would be mature enough for a beach party.

EPILOGUE

After three decades, Talsari beach has its own red crab festivals. These red crabs are called as Red Ghosts by the local humans. They seemed to have changed their habitat by staying awake at night too. Besides scavenging, they hunt small insects if hungry. Tourists and scientists come to see them from all over the world.

The world famous Chilika Lake of Orissa has its own Red Ghosts. Are they native?

2

THE GREAT ESCAPE

Sudha211 and Twinkle338 had always remained thick friends ever since they matured. They had grown up happily in their colony; but now they were slaves.

Sudha211 had to pluck out food items in the jungle, almost five times her body weight and carry it to her colony. At other times she was ordered to suck a honey like substance from inside a fungus and hold it in her crop, which was her second stomach. She was from a brood of Sudha series and hundreds of her sisters with the same name but different numbers had been enslaved and forced to work as worker ants.

Similarly, Twinkle338 along with hundreds of her Twinkle series sisters were forced to work as honey ants. Honey ants would store the honey in their huge crops. Whenever Sudha211 brought honey, she would go straight to Twinkle338 to transfer her honey. The dry food items had to be put in different stores as per their composition.

Well, this was the Ant Colony ruled by Queen Ant Manic.

How Queen Manic and her colony come to Mumbai from Argentina remains a mystery. Some say, that they came inside cargo boxes which had edibles. Her General, Cynti was battle hardy and merciless. Her army wasn't very large but she had a regiment of Commando Ants who could kill several enemy soldier ants without getting seriously hurt.

The Commandos were specially trained to conduct raids and steal the worker and honey ants of other ant colonies. The last raid was in Queen Roopmati's colony, a month ago. Thousands of Sudha series of worker ants and Twinkle series of honey ants were captured from their colony and brought into Queen Manic's colony. They were terrorised and made to obey all orders of General Cynti.

The General was aware that soon Queen Manic would lay hundreds of eggs. Hence more food and workers were required. Thus, the raid.

The worker slaves had to slog day in and day out in the jungles to forage for food. The honey ant slaves were to store the honey safely in their crop till the Queen demanded it, before and after laying eggs.

These eggs would be special as they would produce broods of male ants as well as large female ants. The eggs of both sexes of ants would turn in to larvae when they required special food. Then they would be converted into pupae which would be sleeping all the time. Finally, special groups of male and female ants would come out of the pupae. These 'alates' would come out of the ant hill and, as the Argentine ants had wings, unlike more commonplace ants, would fly off to live together in pairs. They could form many colonies of these aggressive Argentina ants in India. Slowly, the Indian ants who had been living in harmony with the Indian soil, its trees and animals for thousands of years would die out. The Indian ants contributed in many ways to balance Nature and her Eco-systems which were slowly being polluted by humans. They helped in pollination of tiny hills. They also helped in making the soil porous and fertile and spread seeds of very small plants.

No one knew how the Argentine ants would behave.

Twinkle338 had come to know of this plan from a soldier ant who had ordered all the Twinkle slaves not to waste honey as it was required for the Queen and the alates the next day. She had conveyed it to Sudha211 using their special chemicals (called pheromones) based language, through their antenna or even using their forelegs. The soldiers of Queen Manic also passed orders to them in similar pheromones but with subtle differences. These soldiers did not understand the secret language of the slaves.

The next day, deep inside a mangrove forest, Sudha211 met Killa4. Killa4 was a well known scout ant of Queen Roopmati. She would meet Sudha211 quite often to ascertain the developments inside their colony. Very few ants knew that she was a master spy too. Killa4 had hidden from the eyes of Cynti's soldiers, inside a small seed. On learning that the alates were to be born, she gave detailed instructions to Sudha211 to organise a mutiny.

Killa4 and Sudha211 together decided that Queen Manic was to be killed before she could lay her eggs. As she would need large amounts of honey, the Twinkle slaves would be asked to deliver the honey to her; and the assassination was to be carried out at that time. It was expected that General Cynti would be quite disturbed by the death of his Queen. Taking advantage of the situation, Killa4 would launch a surprise attack from outside the next evening. The Sudha series of slaves would be prepared to fight from inside.

Sudha211 quickly moved away from the seed containing Killa4. Besides taking a sip of honey, she also hunted for a special flower. From this flower she took blue pollen and hid it in a tiny blade of grass. She than glued the blade of grass to her thorax.

While returning to the colony Sudha211 conveyed the message by secret pheromones to a few senior Sudha slaves. Inside the colony she went straight to Twinkle338. While delivering the collected honey, she passed on the secret message from Killa4.

Now, Twinkle338 had very little time to plan the killing of Queen Manic. The two friends devised a plan which was to be executed the next afternoon. Sudha221 also handed over the blade of grass containing the blue pollen. This blue pollen was to be stealthily applied by Twinkle338 to Queen Manic while she was taking the honey from her. Very soon the huge and mighty Queen would become weak and could be overpowered by two or three slave honey ants. Her two strong body guards would require some trickery but about eight slave honey ants could easily kill the two.

The next morning General Cynti, as usual, left the colony with her trusted soldiers and slaves to forage for food, water and honey. A little distance away, there was a garbage dump next to a water drain. The drain was broken but it still had some sand and small stones holding the water flow.

Killa4 the spy, had a small commando force of her own. Killa4 wanted to get the force of the worker ants and honey storers who were held as slaves, to be freed. She took the help of Sudha211 by organising a dam burst and a mutiny.

The slaves entered the garbage dump with a few soldiers. General Cynti with some soldiers were guarding them from outside. Killa4 had a small troop of commandos she had brought to the garbage dump. They were hiding in a discarded packet of cheese. Once Cynti had put the workers on their job, she was relaxing with her force, a little away from the drain. Hidden in the cheese packet, behind discarded leaves, Killa4's commandos came out of hiding and removed small pebbles and sand from the edge of the drain. Suddenly the drain water burst, flooding the resting area of Cynti and her force. They were drowned and carried far away from the work place of slaves. It was like the opening up of flood gates. The drain water came out in a strong current and General Cynti and his soldiers guarding the garbage dumps were washed away a long distance. Killa4 and his team soon entered the garbage dump and killed the rest of the soldiers.

The slave workers were very glad with the turn of events. They were all free. Killa4 and Sudha211 explained to everyone that they were to go inside Queen Manic's colony to free the slave honey ants.

Inside the colony, the bodyguards accompanied ten slave honey ants to the queen's chamber. Twinkle338 was the first to enter the dining room. As the Queen started sucking out the honey, Twinkle338 applied the blue pollen to her forelegs. Twinkle339 who was waiting outside also entered the dining room and the two of them overpowered the unconscious Queen.

Then they easily killed her. The eight slave ants outside fought a valiant battle with the two ferocious bodyguards. Twinkle338 came outside and applied the remaining blue pollen on one of the guards who died soon after. But, the other guard killed Twinkle338 before the rest of the slaves could kill him.

By this time Killa4 and Sudha211 with their small rebel army entered the colony. They killed the soldier guards as well as the storekeepers. Sudha211 was heartbroken when she learnt that Twinkle338 had died. The slaves gathered around Killa4 and Sudha211 who were their saviours. Then they marched out to their own colony with the body of their martyr, Twinkle338.

The saviours were honoured by Queen Roopmati.

3

THE TRAIN SINGERS

Rohini was 40 years old when her life was shattered.

Shattered like the windscreen of their car. The thousands of pieces could never be glued together. She was saved by an effective airbag. But her husband, and her daughter just 11 years old, were not saved. Gone forever. Her father, Brijesh, had rushed from Delhi to be beside her in her grief. Her brother, Avinash, was in the United States and would not be able to reach for another week.

Brijesh was keenly aware that a person in Rohini's circumstances may go into deep depression; he even feared that she might attempt suicide. Rohini needed constant attention and care.

Later of course, she would also need a new purpose in life. Perhaps a job or a home-based business might provide a solution. But since Delhi was their hometown and Bhubaneswar was only where Rohini's late husband had worked, it was decided that they go to Delhi at the earliest. Avinash would meet them there.

Soon after the cremation, they packed personal belongings, smaller electronic items and jewellery in suitcases and bags. The furniture, furnishings and other items would be brought by a team of 'Packers and Movers'. Ticket bookings were made on the Rajdhani Express which left Bhubaneswar the next morning for Delhi.

Their luggage was carefully put under the seats. Fortunately, it was midweek and there were fewer passengers in the train. The two were to travel to Delhi in the four-seater cabin which could be bolted from the inside. Brijesh tried his best to engage Rohini in conversation, but it invariably ended in monologue.

"Hopefully this compartment should be ours for the entire journey," said Brijesh trying to engage with his silent daughter.

Rohini remained mute. She did not care to glance at her father as he spoke.

"I need some tea. I'll try to catch the eye of a vendor on the platform," he tried again.

Rohini continue to stare into space, eyes glazed, in a world of her own. Brijesh could not fathom whether she was numb; or indeed, experiencing the agony of her circumstances.

"Time, you know Rohini..." he said gently. "It will take time, but you shall heal. I promise you."

Nothing...

He had bought her some magazines in the hope that she may be diverted, but she didn't read any. He was terribly worried about her mental condition.

The train reached Bokaro railway station at 7 p.m.

Rani, ten years old and Gopi, six years old quietly boarded the train and hid in the enclosure meant for bedding and towels. Once the train left Bokaro, they went about their business of singing songs and begging for alms. A broken sauce pan was the tambourine with Rani, and two flat stones with Gopi, were their musical instruments. Some benevolent people gave them leftover snacks or food. It was their daily routine to board the train at Bokaro at 7 p.m. and alight at Koderma station which the train would reach at about 10 p.m.

They entered Rohini's cabin when she and her father were having their dinner in silence.

Rani sang an old song, "Jo vaada kiya vo nibhana padega..." Once you make a promise, you must fulfil it.

It struck a chord within Rohini, as it was the same song which her husband had been humming when their car met with an accident. Rohini watched continuously while the pair sang and played their 'music'.

"Come here my child," she said.

Brijesh looked up in surprise but was glad that his daughter had spoken.

"Take this," said Rohini to Rani, pressing a 100 rupee note into her palm and gently caressing her face.

"Eat something," she continued, giving the siblings packets of namkeen that her father had packed in the jute bag, which had been placed as to be easily accessible. She split open the two packets for the children.

"Sit down. Finish it."

The waifs ate with relish.

"Thank you, Ma," said Rani, and with a twinkle in her eye, took her little brother and continued to the next cabin to repeat their performance.

Brijesh noted the incident carefully.

At about 9 p.m., the two singers were done with their begging and were returning to their usual hideout. Almost all passengers had bolted their cabin doors. Rohini's cabin door was still open; but she and father had fallen asleep. The children, led by Rani, stepped into the cabin to awaken and alert Rohini; they were well aware that an open cabin door at night did not bode well for passengers.

They heard footsteps.

"Hide... Quick!" whispered Rani to Gopi and both concealed themselves on either side of the door, behind the curtains.

Two persons came in. They switched off the light and bolted the door. One switched on a torch while the other started cutting open the canvas suitcases, one after the other. Rani peeped out and saw them take out jewellery, cash, iPad and some other things she couldn't identify. The robber put it all in a dirty brown bag with a swastika logo. Soon they were done and they walked out, quietly.

Rani had recognised one of them as a waiter of the pantry car because of his uniform.

Not wasting any time, Rani first tried to waken Rohini and then her father, but failed. They were in deep sleep.

"There must have been a sleeping draught in the food brought by the waiter," she thought to herself.

So, she grabbed little Gopi's hand and the two went to a cabin at the rear of the train. It belonged to the Inspector of the Railway Protection Force.

Inspector Thakur looked irate at being interrupted by two urchin children, as he felt that they could be up to no good, and was about to shoo away the duo. However, noting the scared, yet worried expression on Rani's face, he decided to talk to them.

"Now, now you two!" he began sternly. "Why are you wandering around? What do you want with me?"

"Saheb… There has been a robbery. We saw it all. The kind lady and her father were fast asleep. The cabin was not locked. I tried to wake them up to warn them… Just then…" she paused to take a breath.

"Go on," said Inspector Thakur, in a kinder tone as he had guessing that the little girl was speaking the truth and that she might have something serious to report.

"Two men came in…with a brown bag, with a funny symbol on it…cut the luggage…took away money, gold and lots of things, Saheb. One of them was… was…a waiter from the pantry…" she finished in a rush.

Inspector Thakur lost no time. He sent an audio message to his team of constables in the train. Soon, the thieves with the dirty brown bag with a swastika sign on it, were caught.

Inspector Thakur brought the two singers to his cabin.

"Thank you, children. You have been a great help to us. But now, I want you two to come with us to Delhi. The thieves must be punished. I will need you to tell the story to the police."

He also said that the two could sleep in his cabin and all their needs would be looked after by the railways till they reached home by a returning train.

"Ji Saheb," said Rani, feeling slightly bewildered, yet gratified that she could help the police give the thieves what they deserved… Jail!

The children went to sleep.

Early the next morning, Inspector Thakur took the two singers to Rohini's cabin. It took some time for them to wake up. Thakur narrated the happenings of the previous night. He also showed them their suitcases which had been cut open. He reassured them that their valuables were safe with him.

Brijesh thanked the Inspector as he left.

Rohini squeezed Rani's hand.

"Come sit with me," she said her eyes shining. Then she hugged her tightly till the tears cascaded from her eyes down her face. She felt that she was hugging her own daughter who was no more. Then she enquired about her family.

"Where do you live? Why do you sing in the train? Where is your mother?"

"Ma... Gopi and I have no family. We sing for our food and perhaps a little money. We manage to survive..." her voice trailed away.

As soon as Rohini heard that Rani and her little brother were orphans, her eyes lit up.

"Stay with me," she said, holding Rani close. "Both of you." She took Gopi onto her lap. "I will be your real Ma now. You will go to school; I will see that you learn music properly. You will enjoy that. Be my family," she entreated, her eyes reflecting all the love she yearned to shower on the children.

The siblings were overwhelmed by the kindness of the lady. They readily accepted. After all, there was nothing and nobody to go back to! They were homeless orphans with nothing but the to and fro journeys on the Bhubaneshwar-Delhi-Bhubaneshwar train singing for their supper and perhaps a few rupees.

Brijesh was inwardly happy at the sudden turn of events. Rohini had found a new purpose in life...something that she could live for. The grief from her loss could not be wished away; indeed, it would linger for a long time, but its sharp edge would certainly be dulled by her new family. Rohini would find fulfilment and the children would be there for her after he himself was no more.

But yes, he had a lot of work to do. He had to cross many legal hurdles before the adoption could take place. Mere technicalities, though...protocol and procedure... A matter of time.

4

INDRA THE IBIS

Sukma-Dukma dam is located fifteen kilometres East of Babina, a small town in Bundelkhand, India. The dam was built in 1917 on the river Betwa. There is a sparse human population around it. When the water starts receding, just after the rainy season, large flocks of birds arrive here to nest. The Eastern edge of the lake is their favourite as there are tall reeds and swampy soil with an abundance of crustaceans and other insects as food. Palm and other trees are good for nesting.

INDRA'S STORY

I am Indra, a Glossy Ibis. Not truly an Indian citizen. Wise Garuda, our leader, brought us here from Gippsland Lake of Victoria, Australia. I came here along with Sumala, my partner of many years, and our three fledglings who are now independent. I remember the first time we came here, two years ago. I was young and single. Still in the air we could see the azure blue waters of the lake, dazzling in the setting sun. We circled around and landed at the edge of the lake. Having steered us for the 9000 kilometre journey, Garuda asked us to feast upon the insects and small reptiles which were available in plenty. We had not eaten for the last seven days, hence we greedily gorged upon anything that moved. Snails, open shells, dragon flies, tadpoles, chameleons and small snakes were our food. By sunset, we all flew to the nearest tree and huddled together for a deep sleep. Garuda had assigned guard duties to the stronger ones. Otherwise, we would have been easy meat for wild cats. Fortunately, there was a small family of herons and some pelicans on the same tree who were not tired and who would be ready to help.

The next morning, I was up at dawn and flew to the swamp for breakfast. There I spotted Sumala for the first time. She was a beautiful female Ibis. Her beak was brown and sickle shaped. Her body was reddish brown. Her wings were the exquisite colour of bottle green and were tantalizingly glossy. I was bewitched by her. She noticed my steady gaze. We introduced ourselves and had a little chat. I wooed her for a few days. Then, as per our tradition, I built a sturdy nest for the eggs and fledglings. Sumala inspected it and gave her approval. I was the happiest bird that day. Most birds of our flock, a few herons and a couple of pelicans had also built nests on the same tree for their progeny. Two other neighbouring trees had no nests but the adults roosted there. We felt quite secure in such surroundings. The next few months were very tiring for us - first the eggs and then the fledglings.

One night, I was half asleep, near our nest when I heard a twig break. Then another. Was it a jackal? The dry leaves did not make a rustling sound. I reckoned it might be a lighter predator. Maybe a hungry jungle cat. By then, I was wide awake and fully alert. I woke up Garuda and other adults with a special sound which only the Ibis can hear. The cat began to climb our tree. I took flight, made a half circle and dived into the cat. My beak struck its neck and it fell down. The activity in the tree had woken most of the birds; and a cacophony of different bird calls rented the peace of the night. The cat had a partner who was waiting at the base of the tree; who licked the wounded cat. Seeing so many birds ready to attack, they retreated into the darkness, never to return.

In the morning, Garuda praised my courageous act. The wise old bird told us that these were Caracal cats. They could easily jump up to three metres. Normally, they hunted in the drier parts of the jungle; but not having found food there, they had probably strayed to our swampy area. The other parents on the tree were also thankful for my bravery which had saved their fledglings.

Summer had just about started when Garuda announced that we must now migrate to our second home - the scenic Gippsland Lake in Victoria. We were given a fortnight to have a high protein diet and to get fit for the long journey ahead. It would be the first one for our fledglings and I had to give them so many pre-flight instructions. On the night before the journey, Garuda ordered a huddle. We were told to fly in a V formation. Thirteen of us adults were selected for the arrowhead duty as the arrowhead would change twice a day. The flight would take seven days. There would be no breaks for food or water. Just to boost our morale, Garuda told us the story of the Arctic terns who could travel ten times our distance without a break. Their wing span was much shorter than ours.

Miraculous! We thought.

SUMALA'S STORY

We embarked upon our flight without any disruption. After flying around the lake one last time, Garuda took a long, wistful look at our home and spear headed the long flight. Indra and the other stronger ones were next to Garuda. Mothers and those on their first flight were at the two fag ends. Garuda had sufficient experience of wind directions and speed for 'soaring' high with the minimal flapping of wings. As we went higher, he took to the direction of the Indian Ocean. The strong wing flapping of Garuda and those closer to him ensured that others got a lift due to 'wing tip vortex' from the bird. This ensured that those at the tail end spent much less energy during the flight. Garuda also used his navigation sense in the thermal currents of the atmosphere.

On the sixth night, we finally sighted the lights on land. It was near Darwin in Australia. Veer was the arrowhead. Suddenly an aeroplane changed direction and soared high enough to come face to face with our flock. Garuda, who was on the one side of Veer immediately went ahead of him and steered the flock downwards. The whole flock started going down as the aeroplane went upwards. We all had a narrow escape. Veer was very nervous after that close call; and Indra moved forward to become the arrowhead behind Garuda.

But where was Garuda? He was nowhere to be seen. Then realisation dawned upon the leaders of the flock and the rest of us. Garuda had been sucked inside the engine of the aeroplane. He had sacrificed his life to save the flock. My mate Indra kept his cool in this trying circumstance. He steered the sad flock safely to the Gippsland Lake next evening.

The flock landed on the beach; and without a word, went about drinking water and feeding themselves. Indra took the lead in finding their favourite tree. He had become our unannounced leader and I was so proud of him.

5

WINNING AGAINST ALL ODDS

Divya started running, as fast as she could, dodging the morning shoppers in the busy West Street.

"Thief, catch her!" she heard.

She got into an alley before anyone from the crowd could offer a chase. Crossing the Main Street of Pune Camp, she entered into another alley towards the East Street. Panting hard from the strain of the fast sprint, she decided to sit down and catch her breath. She knew that the obese policeman could never catch her. Just when she pulled out the purse she had picked, a wrinkled hand rested on her shoulder.

"My dear little girl, this is my purse. What made you steal it from my pocket?" asked the bald old man.

She couldn't run as he had held her wrist tightly.

"Hunger and poverty," Divya replied blandly, her eyes devoid of any emotion but a tired resignation. "I haven't eaten anything this morning and my mother is bedridden and hungry too," she blurted meekly. Returning her purse, she said, "Please don't hand me over to the police."

"But how could you catch me? You are so old!" she asked with surprise written large on her face.

"Old doesn't mean slow. I am a long distance runner; I also know the streets and alleys of this area very well. But…you need to have some food first. Let's go to Marzipan for a sandwich and a fruit juice. There I need to listen to your story, before I decide what to do with such a young thief like you."

As they sat down to eat, he asked, "How old are you…? And why aren't you in a school?"

"Sir, I am fifteen years old. I was attending the Cantonment school until last year. Class Ten. My father was an alcoholic. He was either late to work or would absent himself, and would get fired. He lost many jobs because of his habit. My mother took up odd jobs as a maid in many homes. One day, my father died by the roadside after a heavy binge at a local bar. My mother made sure I continued to go to school; and I did – for almost two years or so. Then one day at work, she slipped on the soapy floor while washing clothes. She was badly injured and never recovered the use of her legs. Now she is almost bedridden. We had no money for food…so I had no option but to drop out from school. I couldn't get a decent job being a child. As I was a good athlete in school, I thought that picking pockets and disappearing in the maze of alleys was the easiest way to make money," she confessed in a low tone. "What else could I have done?" she queried.

"Hmm" he pondered. Then he said thoughtfully, "Tomorrow, meet me at 5 a.m. sharp in front of the Wanowrie post office. We will go for a run and then decide your fate. My name is Trimbak. I have a daughter, much older than you." As an afterthought, he said, "And yes, take these sandwiches for your mother."

She had not noticed that Trimbak hadn't eaten his sandwiches.

The next morning, Divya waited nervously in the dark for Trimbak to arrive. In a short while, she heard many footsteps coming her way. There were ten of them, all wearing similar sweat shirts with, 'Succour and Soar'. A young lady with Trimbak took her hand and said, "I heard that you are fond of running. I am Jyoti and Trimbak is my father. Join us for the morning run."

Divya had no option but to run with them. Dawn had broken out as they ran next to the centuries old

Banyan trees. They went past the famous AFMC and the Pune Race Club. The air was mystical and a few birds were singing…so peaceful…so invigorating. However, the pace of the group was slow; and Divya was not used to it.

"Why can't we run a little faster?" Divya asked testily. She was used to sprinting in short bursts.

Trimbak cleared his throat and said, "Divya, you are a tigress. The tigress has to feed her cubs. She can go at a tremendous speed but for a short while. The deer on the other hand dodges the tigress. It knows that in a short while the tigress will get tired. We want you to run long. If you run at a slower pace, you can run for a longer distance. You can also keep running into the distant future. Like me…I am over 60 and I run marathon races, that are over 42 kilometres. So, from today, you have to change your pace."

Divya was the youngest of the lot, yet she was tired after just half an hour of the run. Trimbak had sensed it; hence he took a short cut and returned towards the post office. They halted for a while; and then each one handed over a hundred rupee note to Divya.

"Keep the money, Divya. Consider this as an advance. In the evening come to this address and we will talk in detail. Until then, buy some rations. Also buy some books. You will go to school from tomorrow," said Trimbak, as he handed her a visiting card. Then the group left her to herself.

In the evening Divya went to the given address. It was a small office with a board which read 'Succour and Soar'. It was the same name, that was written on the sweatshirts of the runners. Jyoti met her at the entrance. After exchanging pleasantries, Jyoti explained that her father and the other runners were childhood friends. Distance running was their passion. After graduation and getting stable jobs, they had formed this NGO called 'Succour and Soar'. Jyoti was the de facto secretary of the NGO. They supported orphans and other destitute girls. As Divya was a bit educated, she could be put to work as an intern. She had to maintain accounts and in return would get a monthly stipend. She could come on Sundays and holidays for 4 to 6 hours and was free to go to school on weekdays. Every Sunday morning, she had to join the group for a long run! Early morning running was a prerequisite for this intern. The NGO felt that such habits inculcated discipline, ensured work ethics and good health.

TWO YEARS LATER

"You can do it Divya, maintain your pace," came a shout from the crowd. Well wishers from her slum dwelling egged her on, to keep her going.

Divya's legs were tiring but not her brain. She knew that she had to increase her pace in the last 2 kilometres as the sign board read 40 kilometres. There were at least 10 runners ahead of her; but she was determined to come first. The sun was getting harsh and the humidity was draining her energy. Trimbak's running mantra finally gave hope. He had said, "It is not our body which gets tired. It is our mind which tells the body to slow down. If you can keep your mind firm, the body will keep going, as you order it."

She increased her pace by a little bit. The past two years flashed before her eyes. She had cleared her Class 12 Board Examinations. Her mother, having access to Physiotherapy now, was significantly better. She was able to do work of a less strenuous nature; and their joint income had increased. Under Jyoti's guidance, they were eating good nutritious food. Divya had grown taller with strong legs. She could run a half marathon on Sundays with the group, without much difficulty.

Trimbak had seen her potential and had encouraged her to take part in shorter races organised locally, to gain running experience. She was told that she could earn money and get a much better job of she succeeded at the national level in full marathons.

Her tiny hut had posters and cuttings of famous runners like Fauja Singh, Man Kaur, Sunita Godara and Monika Athare. She could relate with Monika as she was the daughter of a very poor person and depended on race prize money for the expensive racing shoes and entry fees for the racing events. Trimbak, however, was her Godfather.

Her father also appeared in her thoughts. He had always chided her for being a good for nothing girl when he was alive. As a girl child she had felt unwanted by him. Further, his alcoholism had meant that she received no fatherly love or support.

Today, she had to prove her father wrong. She wasn't a worthless girl anymore.

Just 3 runners were ahead of her and the last 500 metres board showed up. The cheers of the crowd were deafening. She knew, she had to now run like the tigress if she had to make a kill. She did not see humans ahead of her anymore. They appeared to be deer to her determined, predatory eye. And she moved at a lightning pace to make her kill. She crossed the first one without much difficulty but the second one increased her pace too.

"You can do it Divya!" she clearly heard Trimbak near the finish line.

Finally, she could see the finishing line and tape. Drawing upon her last reserve of energy she almost dived into the tape... If it wasn't for a judge, she would have fallen flat on the ground. Then she passed out.

Jyoti was offering her an electrolyte drink, while Trimbak expressed a sigh of relief when she came to. He was proud of his protégé who had soared. She had stood first in the 'Under-18 Girls' category of the famous Pune Marathon. If she continued to train and run like this, she would be selected for international events and would get a decent job. The prize money would ensure that she could buy better gear and take a stint of professional coaching.

And finally, she felt empowered for a better future. A future without a father.

6

ADITI - THE MOTHER

Shibu, Aruj and Reema, Aruj's wife, were the only tribals in the team of Birju, a sub-contractor. Birju and his team were making a small patch of the national highway crossing the forest of Shivpuri. The Madhavpur National Park was nearby. The forest was being cleared but efforts were made to avoid as many large trees as possible. The trees here were largely of the Sal, Mahua and Tendu variety.

The three tribals were saddened to cut the trees; but they had to earn money somehow! Shibu recollected that as young boys, along with his friends and family, they survived on the forest produce. Leaves of Tendu used for wrapping bidis (Indian cigarette) fetched money. So did the Mahua flowers and seeds. They also collected and sold honey from the bee hives on these trees. The Mahua tree was not only considered sacred but it provided them with many boons. Its flowers, fresh or dried, were edible. They were also used for making a traditional wine. The seeds gave oil which had many uses. Their traditional doctor or vaidya made up to fifty different kinds of medicines from many parts of this tree. That was why, whenever a Mahua tree was cut, the tribals first begged forgiveness.

Birju and the other labourers had no such attachments. They all had set up a camp inside the forest, not far from the proposed highway. Birju had given kerosene oil to these labourers for clearing the undergrowth. Many small reptiles and insects were burnt with the bushes. Even weeds and fungi got burnt. A crow pheasant lost its precious eggs too. However, the tribals ensured that no trees were burnt. They had put up their tent under an old, majestic Mahua tree, whose flowers emitted a very sweet smell in the morning hours.

ADITI THE MATRIARCH

I am Aditi, I am over 300 years old! Well, I am a Banyan tree and with the canopy of my aerial roots I am spread over an acre of land. I was brought by an ascetic, a sadhu, who planted me next to a small temple, that was not much more than a hut. Over these centuries I have seen the temple being destroyed by men on horseback, who also killed the sadhu.

However, I continued to grow and spread. In the last century I witnessed humans coming with saws and chopping down my friends of the Teak and Sal family. They talked of making tracks for the movement of huge iron clad vehicles. I was quite lonely without them after they had been removed; but the mahua trees proliferated. Then a time came when Tendu trees were planted in great quantities around me. I was very happy to have them as my new young friends. They considered me their Matriarch and would look up to me. We would share our knowledge and also our food too. How did we do that?

MEEKA THE NETWORKER

I am Meeka, known to most people as a useless, inedible fungus. A number of us grow in forests, between trees. The ignorant humans are unaware that under the ground I have hundreds of kilometres of networking fibres called mycelium. The scientists call me Mycorrhiza. They have come to learn of my amazing communication skills in the last century. I connect the roots of one tree with another. Generally, I connect trees of the same species but sometimes, I connect interdependent species of trees too.

Trees come to know the requirements of smaller trees and rootlets through me. *And* I have another gift! I can draw water from great depths and transport nutrients through it from the older tree or the mother tree, to the smaller ones. Not only water, I can transport special signals and messages from one tree to another. Very few of these signals are known to the scientists. I have ensured that Aditi, the Matriarch banyan tree is in communication with Mundy, the Mahua's mother tree – the very tree that gives shade to the tents of Shibu and his tribal labourers.

DIWALI NIGHT

The Diwali night was dark. Indians celebrate this festival by letting off a variety of fireworks at night - a practice that has been on for many millennia. Birju and other labourers were no exception. The tribals sang songs to the beat of dholak their traditional drum. Reema could play it very well. Birju fired the last mini rocket which burst into an umbrella of colourful lights. Thereafter, they all went inside their tents.

Unknown to the others, a spark landed next to Mundy. It was still smouldering. The dry leaves and a gentle breeze ignited a small fire. The fire hurt Meeka's mycelium, which went into action immediately. She was aware that Mundy was in danger. Mundy herself was also aware because of her sensors that could discern various odours. Mundy and Meeka wasted absolutely no time. Mundy commenced on her threefold actions. First, she informed forty odd trees which were under her motherly care about her own impending death. Second, she asked Aditi, the Matriarch for all possible help. Aditi could help other trees, even from a longer distance, thanks to Meeka and its brothers. Mundy urged Meeka to pump as much water as it possibly could to her leaves, so that they could become extremely moist and thus resist the flames.

The fire took some time to spread; meanwhile, the humans in the tents had gone to sleep. Shibu was the first to be aware of the smoke. He was alarmed to see the fire. He awakened Aruj. The two of them, broke branches of trees and tried to stamp out the fire. Reema beat her dholak very loudly, so that Birju and other labourers could wake up from their slumber.

Birju immediately took charge. He grabbed the fire extinguisher from his tent and directed the jet of carbon dioxide gas towards the middle of the fire. Other labourers brought buckets of water from the tanker. They threw the water on the sides, preventing it from spreading any further. It took almost an hour for the fire to be totally extinguished.

Mundy was saved but one of her large branches was completely burnt along with its leaves. It would take many years for her to regain her health and balance. However, she would continue to play the role of a mother tree to the others.

The humans would never know what Mundy, Meeka and Aditi had been up to that fateful night. For them, Shibu and Birju had saved their tents from being reduced to ashes. They could never believe that the trees and Meeka had made so many preparations for the fire.

Would you believe it, Reader?

7

RENU AND HER SCHOOL

RENU'S CHILDHOOD

"Mama, it is getting very cold here," complained Renu, "Can't we go somewhere else?"

Renu Gambusia was born in the month of August, when it was extremely hot and humid in the paddy fields of Pilibhit. The rice from this place was famous in the entire region, as were the displaced Sikhs who cultivated the rice. Once the paddy started ripening it was time for the school of Gambusia fish to move into the Gomti river. Every year, the malaria workers brought a few fish from their breeding tanks and put them in the paddy fields when these were full of water.

It was October and the river water was getting colder. Mama Gambusia, the head of this school of fish had decided to go downstream. The Gomti river passed Lakhimpur Khiri, and Sitapur before finally entering Lucknow. Lucknow might be a warmer and nicer place to spend their winter. Once the weather was warmer, they would return to Pilibhit.

"Renu dear, our school plans to leave for Lucknow tomorrow. It won't be this cold there; you and the whole school will have an exciting time. I have heard that the water in Lucknow is quite polluted. The native fish do not go there much. Our school can have as much as we want to eat over there," said Mama Gambusia. "Do you know that our ancestors were brought to India from the US? They lived in a mighty river called the Mississippi. In winters the waters almost get frozen in that river but the summers are just as hot as they are here!"

"But why were they brought here?" asked Renu out of curiosity.

By this time, her friend Raju and many youngsters from their school had joined them and were listening to the conversation very intently.

"Malaria, my dear... This disease killed lakhs of Indians every year. People discovered that mosquitoes spread the disease; so, they began to kill mosquitoes and sleep under nets. Some persons in the US observed that we, the Gambusia fish, were fond of eating the young larvae of the mosquitoes that breed in stagnant water. In fact, we eat larvae of other mosquitoes too, that spread dangerous diseases like Encephalitis, Dengue fever, Filaria and even the new, Zika fever. So, our ancestors were brought to India and were first bred in tanks. Before the start of the monsoons, we would be released in rivers, ponds, cesspools and also into the paddy fields to feed on the larvae."

The next day, led by Mama and a few elders, the school of Gambusia embarked upon their long journey to Lucknow. As their size was small, not more than 3.5 centimetres in length, they stayed away from the deeper waters. What was more, the shallow waters offered them even more food to eat. Apart from larvae of many insects, they ate tiny aquatic beetles and crustaceans. These were animal plankton. The Gambusia also ate vegetable plankton which floated in the waters.

In a few days, the Gambusia school reached Lakhimpur Khiri. At this place, a few tributaries of the Gomti, brought fish from other areas to the river. Shoals of catfish roamed in the deeper waters. One particular catfish had laid its eggs in a small cavity under a stone, in the shallow waters. Mama Gambusia's sharp eyes spotted the eggs. She asked Renu and her young school mates to go and feast on the eggs. She also ordered the adult Gambusia to be around for a possible battle with a much larger fish.

Sure enough, the catfish which had hidden its eggs came to attack Mama Gambusia. Mama Gambusia darted to one side, but five of the adult Gambusia attacked from two sides and brushed their sharp fins on the delicate belly of the catfish. This was done a number of times, causing many small wounds and pain to the catfish. She was quite disabled and gave up the fight. The adult Gambusia hurriedly had their fill. They soon left as fast as they could as they spotted a shoal of catfish coming to help their injured friend. Faster and faster the tiny Gambusia swam till it was dark and time to rest. On Mama's orders the school rested while two guards kept watch over them.

Early the next morning, the school went to the edge of the river to have their meal. Suddenly, Renu, Raju and a few others found themselves suspended in the air, inside a net. As the water flowed down, back into the river, their gills could not breathe. All the Gambusia captured in the net were soon gasping for breath! One of their friends jumped so high that it went out of the net and back to the river. The others were not so lucky, as they were soon put into a box containing water. At least they could breathe now.

What lay in their future?

SOHAN AND RAMPAL

Sohan and Rampal were employees of the Anti-Malaria Department of Sitapur. Their superior officer had tasked them to get Gambusia fish from the Gomti river and release it in the cesspool and ponds of Taaltola mohalla.

It was October and the transmission of malaria had waned away at most places. However, mosquitoes had continued to breed and spread disease at Taaltola. The local citizens had also complained vehemently against the nuisance of the mosquitoes. Hence, their wise old officer had decided to release the Gambusia fish at certain places to eat the larvae of the Anopheles mosquito.

Sohan, the senior of the two, was very happy with the catch as the duo cycled to the vulnerable places where mosquitoes continued to breed.

Renu and Raju were released into a cesspool formed by a broken drain. The place was shady and the water was dirty. The two workers released the rest of the fish in pairs in other drains and small ponds where they saw the larvae. Having carried out their task, they went on to report their success to their superior officer.

The officer was very pleased and hoped that the problem would now be resolved. He was keen on the eradication of Malaria from the mohalla for which he was responsible. A dutiful officer, he wanted no neglect of civic responsibility.

However, Rampal, the new employee innocently asked, "Sir, the waste water in the drains make the cesspool quite dirty and polluted, won't these fish die in a few days?"

"Rampal," the kindly officer began to explain, "these fish are very hardy. They will survive the polluted waters. In fact, they will eat many of the unwanted water insects and vegetation. Secondly, as they are so small, no one will try to catch them for food. So, they will remain safe. Even if the water level becomes very low, they will not die," clarified the officer.

"But sir, if they are so good, shouldn't we breed them and release them into all water bodies," asked Rampal.

"No, Rampal. These fish may be small in size but when they are in a large group in rivers, they are a big nuisance. They are very aggressive; they hurt and kill our bigger sized native fish. They breed very fast and compete for food with our native fish. And...what's more, the number of local fish in our rivers has gone down considerably...which is why, I feel, the Gambusia fish should be used only in ponds, drains and cesspools which have relatively dirty or polluted water in which native fish do not survive," said the old officer as he turned to attend to other tasks.

By Diwali, malaria had almost disappeared from Taaltola. Sohan was returning home in the evening on his bicycle. He got off the cycle to cross the now shallow cesspool where Renu and Raju were released. And…was he pleasantly surprised! Apart from the two adults there were many small Gambusia following them. They had bred so fast!

Renu and Raju were also very proud of their small little school of Gambusia. And what a marvellous journey they had had, from the paddy fields of Pilibhit to the cesspool of Sitapur!

8

BILLY THE RAGPICKER

PART- I

"Hey, that's my bottle, I sighted it first!" shouted Bhura as he snatched the empty beer bottle from Billy's hand.

Billy acquiesced meekly. After all, she was an eight-year-old weakling and Bhura was a ten-year-old bully. Others in their ragpickers' gang were ten-year-old Nashedhi and a seven-year-old Langdi. As their names suggested, Nashedhi could get high on left overs of a cough syrup bottle or near empty tubes of Iodex ointments; and poor Langdi was lame in her left leg.

There had been a fifth, Chhotu, but his fortunes, such as they were, had succumbed to a cruel fate and he had ceased to be a part of the gang.

The foursome scrounged around garbage dumps on the slopes of Shimla hills, enroute to Chadwick Falls. They usually scavenged the sites in close vicinity of hotels and resorts where they could find left over food items. Sometimes they had to shoo off packs of stray dogs and monkeys; it was the survival of the fittest in a jungle-like environment where every mouthful had to be fought for. Finding an empty beer bottle was a luxury as it could be sold for a rupee to Kabadi Chacha, their favourite junk dealer.

The summer season was especially rewarding, as rich tourists threw away half eaten packets of chips and bottles of soft drinks that had gone flat. The ragpickers would provide the lost effervescence with their joy at finding these treasures.

The winters however, were treacherously cold; especially, when it snowed. Huddled together at night they tried to burn the soggy trash with pine tree branches. The skin on their cheeks would turn ruddy with the cold, and was extremely painful to the touch; it would have splits on its surface. Often, they had to sleep hungry.

One of their members Chhotu, had tried to make money by begging outside the Lakshmi Temple. He had soon been picked up by the begging mafia. Stone-hearted and merciless, they had maimed him for life. Subsequently, he had been made a part of the organised business of begging. Last heard, he was crying for alms outside the Tara Devi temple.

Some nights, Billy remembered her mother. Her mother came to soothe her after a nightmare haunted her in the middle of the night. The nightmares had begun when Billy was just four years old.

Her father, a truck driver would come home drunk, late in the night, every three or four days, from an outstation trip. Her mother would ask for money to keep the hearth burning and he would become abusive; often, he would get violent and thrash her. Billy would wake up, sobbing. These scenes were etched on her brain.

One day, out of the blue, he brought new clothes for the two of them and took them for a ride in his truck to the hills. Her mother Mani was thrilled at the apparent change of heart of her husband. A simple lady, she asked no questions, going along with the surprise adventure. They reached Dhali, at the outskirts of Shimla, late in the evening. They had a sumptuous meal at a nearby dhaba, a poor man's restaurant. Then, they went to sleep on the roadside, under the stars. Early morning, when Mani and Billy woke up, there was no truck and no father. Both seemed to have vanished into thin air! They walked in all directions, looking for the truck but it was nowhere to be found. They were in tears.

Mani was now homeless and penniless with a little daughter in tow. She went around the numerous dhabas and tea shops begging for food for hungry Billy. She even offered to wash their utensils but to no avail. Finally, when she was at her wit's end, an elderly dhaba owner took pity on them and let her in. Mother and daughter were given food and shelter on the condition that she would cook meals for customers and wash utensils. Mani agreed with alacrity. They were also given shelter inside the dhaba at night. Finally, the duo had a roof over their heads, and Mani had a job to keep herself and her little child.

The arrangement seemed to work very well for a month as the number of customers increased because of the lady's touch in the meals. Mani was generously given some money to buy new clothes and other essentials. Billy would play indoors and became familiar with the dhaba uncle. Mani told Billy to address the dhaba owner as Papaji.

One day, Papaji asked Mani to look after the dhaba, while he took Billy to Sair Mela, an annual fair, for fun and to purchase some spices. The walk was long and tiring but Papaji bought her ice cream which she ate, sitting on a bench. Having walked for over an hour on the cart road they continued on their way downhill, till they finally reached the mela site. At the mela, Papaji bought her red ribbon and bangles. He also paid for rides on the merry-go-round. When Billy got off the merry-go-round, there was no sign of Papaji. Billy started running here and there, looking for him frantically. She didn't know his name. She did not know the way back to the dhaba. Soon, it began to grow dark. Visitors were beginning to leave and so were the handcarts.

That was when she met Bhura and Nashedi. They offered solace to the tearful girl. She found comfort in the company of the other children who also seemed to be alone, devoid of adult supervision. In a short while, developed a friendly rapport, one that had sprung from utmost purity of feeling; and went to look for dinner below a resort where plentiful garbage would be regularly dumped. They were able to satiate the almost painful pangs of hunger.

In a matter of days, they shared their stories.

The boys were beaten by their step mother or father and had just run away from the village. The ragpickers' gang grew larger when Chhotu and later Langdi joined them. It was a new life. Scavenging for meals. Lucky to find some empty bottles or other stuff to sell to Kabadi Chacha. Sleep under the stars. The air in the garbage dumps was putrid but it smelt of freedom. No more abuses or beatings by elders.

PART II

Balwinder was the first to be called to receive her Degree at the Convocation held at the Palampur Agriculture University. She had topped the Biotechnology course and was soon to leave for Stanford, California. She had opted to study and research Waste Disposal and Climate Change in the United States.

After the function, she paid a visit to Krishnapur, her 'home'. She touched her Gram Mata's feet with reverence. The Gram Mata was proud of her protégé's achievements and showered her with blessings. Then Balwinder went to her dormitory to just lay on her bed, tired from the hectic proceedings of the day.

As she shut her eyes, she transformed into an eight-year-old Billy.

A thin, dirty Billy in torn clothes. She distinctly remembered the day she and Langdi had been captured in a raid by some social workers. The two teenage boys of the ragpickers' gang, had been too fast for these workers. Both girls were taken to some girls' hostel, bathed, given new clothes and food.

Later, they were brought to a large hall and made to sit with another five boys and girls on the stage. They were seven children in all – ragpickers or beggars or day labourers, freed by social workers. A team of officers and a distinguished gentleman came onto the stage. They addressed the gathering and the press. A mature lady called the Gram Mata was also present. They were photographed and later sent to Krishnapur with the Gram Mata.

Krishnapur was a tiny village, and Gram Mata, its head. She took the newcomers under her wing. A motherly figure, she never asked them any embarrassing questions. She had only showered them with her love and told them that she was always free to meet them individually in her room.

They lived in their dormitories – separate ones for boys and girls. They all dined together, prayed together and studied together till they were old enough to join a regular school in Class Seven. Here she was enrolled as Balwinder, a new name, she had chosen for herself. Langdi was also called by her new name – Lakshmi. She was a year junior to her but they remained thick friends.

Nights continued to disturb her. Mother still came in her dreams. Occasionally she had nightmares of her violent father too. Sometimes, she wondered why she was abandoned by her Papaji at the mela. But daytimes were much better. With no fear of having to hunt for her next meal, Balwinder had grown immersed into her books. In her spare time, like others, she cleaned their dormitories and did the kitchen duties too. Sundays were spent in washing and ironing clothes. Evening prayers with the Gram Mata were mandatory for everyone and so was morning yoga. Except for a few new boys, most of the others had understood the value of this community living. They all revered the Gram Mata as their Fairy Godmother.

"Get up for prayer, Billy," shouted Lakshmi.

Later, after dinner, the Gram Mata called Balwinder to her room. She said, "Tomorrow you will leave the village. You will go to Delhi for your flight. But why are you going to Shimla first?"

"I have some unfinished business at Dhali. A tea shop owner got separated from me at a mela twenty years ago. I want to meet him and ask him – 'Did you leave me deliberately on the merry-go-round?'" replied Balwinder as she walked away, hiding her tears.

9

KAMINI'S YELLOW ARMY

PART – I

ANIK'S ANGER

"Oh Mummy!" cried Anik, "I am being bitten by wasps."

Savi, his elder sister wiped his tears and together with Anurag, their friend, quickly brought him down the staircase. They were playing hide and seek on the rooftop garden. Anik went to hide behind a bamboo curtain next to the staircase wall. He had accidentally touched the nest of the yellow paper wasps. Lo and behold, a whole army of these yellow coloured wasps, led by Bela attacked him with all their might. They stung him on his face, neck and hands till he ran away crying for help.

He now lay on his bed, his mother applying a soothing cream. He had already gulped a pain reliever and an anti-allergy tablet. The sting marks continued to swell. It would take at least four or five days to subside.

The next day, sitting on the bed, he was still feeling peeved. Anurag had come to visit him.

"Anurag, listen…" he whispered.

"I am in so much pain…I will take revenge on these wretched creatures, so that such an attack doesn't happen again. If they stung me once, they can sting any of us at any time…Just think…it could be Savi, or even you! You have absolutely no clue the agony! You will help me."

"How?" said Anurag, simultaneously outraged at the attack and excited at the thought of adventure.

"We'll burn down their nest. Silly papery thing! That will put an end to this nuisance!"

Anik thought that the wasps were useless pests. He also hated the honey bees; but then, they produced honey which he loved.

Saturday night was fixed as the night of the attack.

"We will need a cloth rag tied to a stick; and we will flick a bottle of kerosene from the kitchen," said Anik. "And according to my plan," he continued, "We will burn down the nest when the wasps are asleep."

"And to protect ourselves, we will use our hoodie jackets, plain glasses, masks and leather gloves," added Anurag with a sly grin on his face.

Excitement was building up – but secrecy was maintained from the parents.

PART – II

BELA'S STORY

Bela was just a carnivore soldier of Kamini's army of yellow paper wasps. Kamini had singlehandedly built the paper nest using wood from the door and her own saliva. This was an art which only the 'foundress' female wasps like Kamini knew. Then she had laid eggs for a brood of sterile female worker wasps, like Bela. Later she laid more eggs for female wasps who could bring back food for her. She needed extra diet to produce more larvae in the near future. Some of the food would be stored.

A few of the female wasps were capable of becoming new Foundresses who could set up new nests. But for that, Kamini had to lay special eggs which became male wasps. As a queen, nature had bestowed this power of controlling the sex of her offspring. This was Nature's way of ensuring continuity of their species. Once the male eggs matured into adults, they could mate; and the male adults die soon after mating.

Bela and the other workers helped maintaining nests and keeping enemies like Anik away. As they were very active, they constantly searched for sugar like food and water. Nectar or honey dew on flowers was their favourite but they didn't mind fruits or even the sweets eaten by humans. Bela and her worker wasps lived on the outer hexagonal chambers of the nest.

The wasps who brought food entered the inside of the nest to deliver the food and the nectar to other wasps who stored it. In the middle of the nest was Kamini, in a vacant chamber where she laid eggs. These eggs matured into larvae.

When Anik had come close to their nest, Bela and other soldiers had encircled him as a warning. But Anik's accidental touch of their nest was an act of war. Bela and her fellow soldiers swarmed on the bare parts of his body stinging him many times.

Bees can sting only once as their stinger breaks away. The wasp stinger doesn't break and each wasp can sting many times causing immense pain and misery. Only when their enemy admitted defeat and ran away from the battle field, did Bela and her fellow soldiers return back to the nest.

PART – III

UNCLE ASHOK, THE AGRO SCIENTIST

On Saturday evening, Uncle Ashok dropped by to enquire about Anik's wellbeing. He was a close family friend, who worked as a scientist in the Horticulture department. Anik, Savi and their mother welcomed Uncle Ashok. As their father had just returned from his jogging routine, he was having a shower. Their mother also went to the open kitchen to make Ashok's favourite 'masala chai'.

"How are you feeling today?" asked Ashok.

Anik replied, "Much better, Uncle. But these good for nothing wasps are simply horrible." Then in a low whisper he said, "Anurag and I plan to burn down their nest tonight. But please don't mention anything to my parents."

Ashok looked directly into Anik's eyes and said softly, "Wasps are predators. They are like spiders, lizards, frogs, snakes, wolves and tigers. They play a great role in maintaining ecological balance. Do you know, once wolves were hunted and killed in the 17th century? It happened in the USA when the European settlers raised cows. The wolves would come at night and kill the cows for food. The cowboys started killing the wolves…until one day, there was not a single wolf in the Great Yellowstone Park."

"What happened then?" asked Savi, curiously.

"The number of deer and rabbits increased tremendously. They ate away most of the grass, small plants and bushes, especially near the water streams and rivers. Because of this, the soil from the river banks began to erode away. Then the rivers started flooding. The land on the plains had no grass or bushes. Many animals died because of floods. Over two hundred years later, scientists advised the government to reintroduce wolves in the park. In just two decades the park regenerated. Tall trees, bushes, grass and wild flowers came back. So did many animals. The deer and the rabbit populations decreased and they found safer places to live but away from the water sources. Flooding was much less," he replied.

By then Savi's mum had served tea. She disliked lizards and Uncle Ashok continued with his lecture, "Do you know, if there were no lizards and spiders in our home, what would happen?"

"Our house would be full of flies and mosquitoes. Our wooden doors and windows would be eaten by tiny pests. We would have huge cracks in our floors and walls because of various pests. There would be cockroaches everywhere. These insects and pests are the food of lizards and spiders," he explained.

Anik could not resist chiming in to say, "But uncle, wasps are useless. We must kill all the wasps."

Ashok replied calmly, "No my child. God has given each creature a role to play in nature. Wasps have many roles to play, but people are unaware of them. First, they kill many small pests in your mama's kitchen garden as well as in farms. These pests are capable of destroying the crops. They also kill caterpillars and other harmful insects and keep their population under control. Otherwise, the caterpillars would eat leaves and flowers of plants, ultimately killing them. Secondly, wasps pollinate certain small flowers which the bees do not visit because of their peculiar smell. The so-called weeds of these small flowers hold soil together. Another species of wasps is really very interesting. But first you must know that fig fruit has flowers inside the fruit. So how are they pollinated? Well, a special wasp bores a hole in the fig when it is small. As it enters it, it loses its wings. Inside the fig, it goes from one flower to another, sucking nectar and carrying pollen on its body. It also lays its eggs inside the fig, some eggs become larvae too. Then the wasp dies inside the fig. Once the larvae mature to adults, they mate. Then the males make a hole and the female wasps come out while the males die. So, if it weren't for these wasps, there would be no figs either."

Savi gave a mischievous glance towards Anik and said, "So Anik, now you know, if it wasn't for the wasps, mama wouldn't be able to give yummy tomatoes and cucumbers for your salad. Moreover, so many flowers would feel unhappy if there weren't any wasps. You still feel like burning down their paper nest?"

Anik could only grin sheepishly.

He had developed a new respect for wasps. He felt that it was his responsibility to remain away from them.

10

BOYS WILL BE BOYS: SHOULD THEY BE?

"Hello, Sangram, I have not heard from you for a week. Is all well?" Vijay asked his long time college friend. Both hailed from North India and had come to work in the metropolitan city of Mumbai. Sangram was living with his office colleagues in an independent flat. Vijay was staying in a smaller place just above his office.

"No um... come soon," replied Sangram and he hung up.

Sangram was a wrestler of some repute, and his voice had been barely audible. Vijay called again, several times; but Sangram did not reply. Now Vijay was worried. It was the first Sunday after the Lockdown had been announced by the Prime Minister. A new disease had come from China spread by a deadly Coronavirus, for which there was neither prevention nor cure. Everyone was confined in their homes. However, on Sunday a half day was given for the shopping of essential items and food. Could Sangram be suffering from this disease? Vijay was a conscientious person. He decided to pay his friend a visit.

After buying his weekly groceries, Vijay went to Sangram's flat. No one answered the doorbell. He was now quite disturbed. So, he opened the flat with a spare key given by Sangram. As he entered inside, he saw Sangram sprawled on the sofa, his cell phone on the floor. Vijay checked his pulse. It was fast and weak. Even his eyes were sunken and his unshaven face looked dehydrated. He knew what to do in such an emergency. Immediately he went to the kitchenette and put two tea spoons of sugar and a pinch of salt in a glass of water. As he stirred it, he remembered how to make oral rehydration solution, also called ORS. His father, a male nurse in the armed forces had taught him, when his younger sister had loose motions. "No one dies of loose motions my son; they die of dehydration. Just keep feeding them this ORS," he had said.

Vijay force fed ORS to Sangram after lifting his head up. Sangram drank a few sips. In a minute or so, his eyes opened and Vijay made him drink the whole glass as fast as he could.

"Oh Vijay, thanks," was all that he said.

Vijay now surveyed the house. The living room was a mess. Unwashed dishes and banana peels were left on the table. Unwashed clothes were piled in a corner. The kitchenette was also unkempt. Vijay first cleared the counter and washed some dishes. He made another glass of ORS, this time squeezing a small lemon into it. He gave it to Sangram who was quite alert now, but still too weak to stand up.

"So, Sangram. Tell me what happened; and where are your flat mates?" asked Vijay.

"Oh, Sunil and Anant... They both come from Igatpuri. On hearing the PM's speech, they both rushed off to their native place. I was left alone. I've been all by myself since that day. I don't know how to make an omelette or cook Maggi. However, I can boil eggs and make coffee. So, I had bought a loaf of bread, some bananas and eggs. Those finished yesterday morning. I tried making some Maggi but it turned out so mushy that I had to throw it away. Since then, I have not eaten anything. Just drinking coffee," replied Sangram.

Vijay was perplexed on listening to this. He further probed, "But how were you managing until now?"

“Well, Sunil has a passion for cooking. He makes the dinner. Lunch is from the Dabba wallahs. Breakfast is simply bread, butter and boiled eggs,” said Vijay.

“Why didn’t you ever learn basic hygiene like cleaning up your place or washing your clothes or making a peas pulao? These things are so simple.” queried Vijay.

“Now Vijay, I was the only son in our joint family. My mother had given strict instructions to all females of the family to do my work. I never polished my shoes or put out my wet towel in the sun to dry. I was told that boys and men don’t do domestic work. Period,” said Sangram proudly.

“But how did you survive the hostel?” asked Vijay.

“My father had given me large bag and sufficient clothes. I would bring them home every Saturday night. For any other need I just rang them up and it was met,” he said.

“Wait then, I will make some Khichdi for you. It will give you strength and nourishment,” Vijay concluded and went to the kitchen.

He opened his shopping bag and took out some peas, carrots and potatoes. After cleaning and chopping them, he put them in a pressure cooker with rice, yellow lentil, salt and turmeric. He then added water and put it on the pressure cooker. As he was chopping cucumber and tomatoes for the salad, his mind went back to when he was ten years old.

"Vijju," said his father politely, "Please pick up your used plate from the table and put it in the kitchen sink. While coming back, bring the duster and wipe the table clean."

His mother had immediately said, "Let his sister Neera do it. After all, he is a boy."

"No," his father had said firmly. "We will treat both of them in a similar manner. Later, he will go to a hostel and then get a job. Will you send Neera or will you go there? Vijju is old enough to learn 'Self Care Skills'. By the time he leaves us, he should be able to manage by himself."

'Toot toot' blew the pressure cooker's whistle. Back to present. He thought that it was time for Sangram to learn the 'Self Care Skills'. He couldn't remain a typical Indian boy for ever.

Vijay served the steaming Khichdi with a dollop of butter, salad and yoghurt. Sangram ate the delicious meal in silence. Vijay also joined him for this impromptu meal on the sofa. After the meal, Sangram quietly took the plate from Vijay and went to the sink. Seeing the clean kitchen, he felt guilty and began to wash the used utensils.

When he had finished, he said quite meekly, "I am extremely thankful Vijay. I am strong enough. But I want you to stay here. No, it is not that I want you to cook meals for me. I want you to teach me the basics of cooking."

Vijay replied, "Friend, I can't leave you in this condition. However, if I stay back, I have to be here till the next Sunday when Lockdown is relaxed for shopping. I haven't brought any clothes either. I have to buy groceries too. The ones I had bought for myself, I will leave with you. But yes, your cooking classes start from this evening. Online. You set up your laptop in the kitchen and I will guide you, step by step. Before I leave, promise me one thing."

"Anything bro. You just tell me what is it?" asked Sangram.

"Well, the fact is that your whole flat is stinking and dirty. Promise me that you will clean up the flat and wash your clothes. Not just today, but every day. In case you have an issue, just let me know," said Sangram.

As he left, he silently thanked his father for being firm in his boyhood, for making him a complete person. Unlike Vijay, who, for so long believed in the maxim - Boys Will Be Boys!

11

BASANTI AND HER BROOD

BASANTI'S STORY

Basanti the unique carefree creature was an expert swimmer and a tree lover.

When not swimming in the little stream full of vegetation, she would be lying lazily on the branch of a tree. She could go without meals for many weeks or months depending on what her last meal had been. Her friend and neighbour, Jay had once swallowed and constricted a calf. After that he slept like Kumbhkaran for six whole months.

Well, after all, they were Indian pythons – Python Molurus, non-venomous reptiles. Basanti was around five metres long, weighing around fifty kilograms. She was mud coloured with greenish brown patches. With such colours, she could merge with her surroundings very well.

Today, Basanti was hungry. Lying on the tree trunk she had noted a plump bandicoot the night before. Not finding grains or vegetables to eat in the nearby village, the bandicoot was gnawing away at the bark of the tree.

"How dare he?" thought Basanti. "It will weaken my beautiful tree!"

Rodents like rats, mice and bandicoots multiplied too fast. They ate practically everything in sight. They even carried many disease-causing insects on their body hairs. Nature made reptiles to keep their population in check. Reptiles ate other small animals like frogs and rabbits. Pythons, usually larger than snakes swallow and crush larger animals like deer and calf.

"I shall eat this bandicoot…in the wee hours of tomorrow morning," thought Basanti and looked forward to her next meal. Smacking her chops, she set herself to bide her time.

Late in the evening, Basanti slithered off the tree to the dense grass next to the tree trunk.

The bandicoot came in the night, as Basanti had expected it to, and went about its job merrily, blissfully unaware of its fate. Late in the night, he had finished his meal and was taking a rest.

In the darkness, the two thermo-sensors in the pits of Basanti's head were transmitting all movements of the bandicoot to Basanti's brain. Only when she sensed 'no movement' of her prey, she struck swiftly. Her special, huge jaws opened up and grasped the bandicoot's head. Her tail coiled around firmly on the body of this creature. The four rows of teeth in her upper jaw and two rows in her lower jaw, all facing inwards, ensured that the prey could only go inside her body. The constricting hold of a python's body and tail is so strong that even a deer cannot free itself.

Usually, pythons have their own territory and they avoid other pythons and their territories. Basanti also did not have any friends. But that winter, she had an urge to have her own brood of tiny pythons. So she went to her neighbour, Jay for a few days of togetherness and mating. Thereafter, she returned to her favourite spot, by the stream. In a month's time, she laid fifty white, speckled eggs which had a leathery feel. She coiled around the eggs, giving them her body's warmth. When it was cold in the night, she would shiver deliberately. The shivering would maintain the required temperature. It made her tired and hungry. However, there was no time for food till the eggs hatched. One sunny day, she felt the need to warm her body in the sun. The eggs would also remain warm in the sunlight, she thought, as she lay comfortably.

BUNTY AND HIS TEAM

Bunty lived in a village on the Bareilly-Nainital highway. His 'Under-18' football team was practising for the district tournament. Recently, their playground next to the highway had been taken over by a trust that had planned to open a medical college.

Bunty's team was extremely disappointed by this development; and being passionate about football they cleared some barren land next to the stream and resumed their practice.

On that fateful day, Basanti was lying half asleep when the football rolled near her. Bunty appeared, running after the ball. He was terrified by the sight of this enormous python. Who would not be?

He rushed back in fear shouting, "Snake! There's a huge snake! It's like a monster! We need to do something, or we will surely die!"

The friends armed themselves with lathis and encircled Basanti from all sides. Poor Basanti was no match for the physical assault by several young but strong village lads, as she was being beaten black and blue. Unable to move, she prayed for her brood of eggs.

Hearing the commotion, a wise villager, Ajay, came running to the spot. He was a laboratory technician in the reptile division of Indian Institute of Veterinary Sciences, IVRI. This institute was located at Izzatnagar, a few kilometres from their village. He immediately identified the injured python.

"Stop children, stop!!" he cried with urgency. "This snake is not venomous! I should know...believe me!"

The boys drew back and while they still held on to the lathis, they stopped hammering poor Basanti. After all, this was Ajay, and he would know more than anyone else in the village!

"This python is every farmer's friend. It eats rodents and other pests and protects our crops. Let me take care of this."

Ajay also discovered the eggs, which fortunately were safe. He then rang the IVRI emergency department for an ambulance. The boys of the team helped lift and transport Basanti and her eggs to the reptile section where Dr Ajmal Khan, Reptile specialist Veterinary Surgeon took Basanti under his care. He nursed her wounds carefully. The eggs were put in an incubator. In ten days' time the eggs hatched and fifty cute baby pythons emerged. The hard-working doctor also ensured that Basanti was fine by now. The brood was brought to Basanti.

Was she proud and glad to see the young hatchlings?!

Bunty and his team had realised their folly and felt guilty about the whole episode. Ajay helped them gain first-hand knowledge about reptiles in general, but pythons in particular.

Dr Khan had a special task for them.

"Listen boys… There is something you can do for the python community. Are you willing to help?"

The boys nodded their assent.

"Python skin is a prized product in the fashion capitals of the world. It is used to make purses, bags, shoes and belts. These are sold at exorbitant prices…and you know what? The skin is smuggled out from our country. Sometimes a live python's skin is removed for even more money. It is cruel and illegal. Man's greed knows no bounds. You can see the problems the world is facing today from the gradual destruction of Nature. It is wrong!" So saying, he advised the youths to help preserve our pythons.

Bunty and his team decided to form a 'Save our python' group. They went from one village to another, educating the people. The villagers were told about the harmless nature of pythons and how they helped the farmers and protected crops and other vegetation. They also helped the IVRI team with the release of Basanti and her brood to her 'kingdom' by the stream. In a few months many of the tiny pythons would migrate along the stream to set up their own domain.

Bunty and his team vowed to look up Basanti and her brood every Sunday.

12

JEEVA AND BHIMA OF HOLLONGAPAR

At just six months, Jeeva's hair had started turning black, just like his father's body hair. Earlier, his body hair was like his mother's – beautiful, soft fur of buff colour. She had cuddled him and carried him for almost six months, jumping from branch to branch and even while he was sleeping.

Now he was being trained by his father, jumping by himself from branch to branch, very carefully. They would train in the late night and early morning. Later, they would be asleep on the tree tops.

Fruits, flowers and if lucky, some bird's eggs were their food. They were a small family of Indian Gibbons, a variety of apes, who lived in the Hollongapar Reserve Forest of Assam. This forest was the only one of its kind in India. The forest was so named because of the 150 feet tall Hollong trees.

Jeeva had a few friends who lived atop these tall trees, nearby. They were used to living comfortably on the top of these trees. Bheema was another young Gibbon who would often come to his tree to play with him from a nearby tree top.

One day Jeeva's 25-year-old grandfather sat next to the two of them. He narrated to the two youngsters the long history of the special apes of the tree tops, The Gibbons. The young ones listened with rapt attention. Grandfather told them that the tall Hollong tree on which they lived had three tiers. They lived on the highest tier. In the middle tier were the capped langurs and hill macaques. On the bottom tier were the common rhesus monkeys or the bandoors as the Assamese people called them. The bandoors could hop on the ground too. Some bandoors had made friends with the forest guards who lived at one end of the forest. The guards would feed the friendlier ones with food too. Once in a while the bandoors went to the nearby tea planters' colony for food. But one young bandoor was caught and taken in a truck to a faraway land. The young gibbons were never to go down to the lower tiers.

On another day, Grandfather told them stories which his grandmother had told him. She had said that in their times, the forest had been very huge. Elephants would take months to travel from one end to another. There were no tea gardens. Rainfall was heavy most months of the year and there was no shortage of food. Then… the white men came and cut the forests. Tea gardens came up, huge trains and trucks also drove in. Thousands of tigers, rhinos, leopards, pangolin, bears, flying squirrels and birds died when the trees were cut as they lost their home and habitat. Many others were hunted for meat or making medicines. The Gibbons were on the verge of becoming extinct, when Jeeva's grandfather was born. Just then some wise people realised their folly. They began planting trees and prohibited entry of humans into their forest. Trained guards were employed to protect them. For this reason, they should never leave the forest, not for any reason whatsoever, as other humans might kill them.

The fun filled days of Jeeva and Bhima appeared to be coming to an end. Rainfall had been very scanty; new shoots and flowers on the tree tops had dwindled in their numbers. The birds too, had migrated to distant places.

The two friends had matured considerably and their arms were as big and as strong as those of their parents. They had learnt to forage food on their canopy at the tree top. Thus, they needed more food now than earlier, but adequate food was difficult to come by. They had been to numerous treetops in their neighbourhood, but food was scant everywhere. The langurs would often go down to the bandoors' tree tier. The bandoors had begun to frequent the tea garden camps hoping to raid kitchen gardens and garbage dumps.

One day the two friends had to go without food. Late that night Bhima suggested to Jeeva that the two should also go to the tea garden camp with the bandoors. They could leave in the hours of darkness and come back by sunrise. Jeeva was afraid in the beginning – he remembered his grandfather's warning. But the hunger in his stomach willed him to agree to Bhima's suggestion.

Before dawn, the two friends sneaked down, one tier to another, till they were on the ground. They were very excited to touch the earth for the first time in their lives. They noticed four bandoors going out of the forest. They followed the bandoors till they reached the tea garden camp. Here, one bandoor went towards the kitchen garden while three bandoors and the two friends tried their luck in the garbage dumps behind one house. They were busy enjoying a feast of over ripe plums, when suddenly a window opened and sacks fell over Jeeva and Bhima. Bhima was fast enough to throw the sack off but Jeeva was caught in it. Afraid, the bandoors and Bhima fled from there to the nearest tree. Two men jumped out from the window, tied the sack with Jeeva in it and took him inside.

On the tree, Bhima was heartbroken. He spoke with the bandoors in sign language that he needed their help to save Jeeva. Upon receiving the message, one of the older bandoors left the group and ran towards the forest. The other two bandoors agreed to help. They sat on the roof of the house, while Bhima hid himself on a tree in front of the main door of the house.

A century ago, Gibbon meat was a delicacy amongst the local tribals. The forest cover was quite thick then and the Gibbon population was quite large.
They were also in great demand in China. Gibbons' fur was used by the rich Chinese to make fashionable and expensive clothing. Some of their body parts and bones were used to make traditional Chinese medicines. But the most expensive thing was the Gibbons' fresh blood which was mixed with wine. Chinese people drank this concoction as they believed it to be an elixir of youth. They desired to remain young.

Hence the poachers, for that was what the men were, were ecstatic to have captured a live Gibbon. Jeeva was lucky to be alive. But sitting inside a dark sack made him restless and unhappy. He felt angry at himself for not obeying his grandfather's warning. He desperately wanted to go back to his mother's lap and cry.

In a little while, as the sun was rising, a jeep approached the house. Bhima and the two bandoors were alert now. Two men came out of the house with the sack and were about to get into the jeep. Just then, the three apes pounced! The two bandoors, each jumped on a man's neck. Bhima with his strong arms, snatched the sack from the startled men and ran away. Just then, the jeep driver stepped out with a gun in his hands.

BANNGGG! He shot at Bhima but missed…as Bhima went behind a bush, with the sack in his hands.

In the meantime, two forest guards arrived on a motor cycle. Their third bandoor friend was sitting on the shoulder of one of the guards. They fired a warning shot and asked the poachers to surrender. The two bandoors, perceiving that help was at hand got to the ground and stood behind the poachers as guards, but snarling all the while. Only when the poachers had been tied, did the three bandoors leave. Bhima emerged from the sack and muttered a thank you.

Then they all fled as fast as possible to their home tree. They had learnt their life's lesson that day.

'Gibbons never get down from the Hollong tree'.

***

POSTSCRIPT

Gibbons play a special role in ensuring seed dispersal of the unique tall trees where they reside. The Indian Gibbons are an endangered species. International Gibbons' Day is celebrated on 24th October each year.

13

THE DEAD TREE

One summer, my wife and I came to Hyderabad to meet our daughter and her family. As my son in law is an army officer, they were at the time, living in an old bungalow surrounded by a dense thicket of trees and vegetation. Nitty and Amy, my twin granddaughters were 10 years old.

We sat relaxing in the front lawn when I asked, "Such a beautiful lawn and a garden you have, what is the dead tree doing there, next to the neem tree?" I pointed to the tree I was referring to. "Shouldn't your father get it chopped and utilise the wood for some useful purpose?" I continued.

"Oh Nanu (grandfather), this tree is not really dead. Wait until tomorrow morning and see the magic. But get up early and don't leave the verandah. More importantly, don't make much noise," instructed Nitty.

Early the next morning, I was awakened by the calls of a peacock. I quickly freshened up and sat on the porch swing. Soon enough the twins came and sat on either side of me. All three of us focused our sights on the dead tree. The muster of peacocks had disappeared by now. A mongoose ran outside and disappeared behind the bushes. We could hear the chirping of hungry young birds. A pair of parakeets landed on the dead tree. One sat on the top branch and another disappeared to the back side of a large branch.

"Nanu, they are Mr and Mrs Hooks, the parakeets. Their young ones are in a hole facing the fence. Mrs Hooks has brought worms to feed her young ones. Mr Hooks is keeping guard from the highest branch," explained Amy in a very low tone.

In a little while, as we sat silently, Gossipy Mynahs came to feed their brood. The young ones of mynahs were quite loud and made a variety of sounds. A squirrel scampered up the tree with a beetle in its mouth. A moth came from somewhere and hid in the crevice of the bark which was hanging loose.

As I enjoyed the scene, Nitty began her long lecture, "Preethi ma'am, our science teacher told us that under the barks and inside the hollows of dead trees live thousands of different kinds of creatures. There are insects like beetles, carpenter bees, wood wasps, weaver ants, spiders, carpenter ants, borers and termites. Moths and butterflies come to rest. Predators like chameleons, birds, tree flying squirrels, bats and snakes come to feed. Wood peckers communicate with each other by striking on the hollow branches. The holes they create are used by many birds, to lay their eggs, especially the parakeets. If there were no dead trees the parakeets would disappear. Most of these species have nowhere else to go and live in harmony with each other...except on such dead trees. In many countries, the dead trees were removed from the forests leading to a loss of species."

'Child is the father of a man,' said a wise man. Today, my grandchildren were teaching environmental science!

"Nanu, look at the beautiful pair of hornbills sitting majestically on the top branch now," said Amy. It was her turn now as a pair of sun birds also rested for a while and darted towards a flying bee. Drongos came for the same purpose. The barbet sat hidden from us but its copper smith like 'tuk-tuk call gave her away.

We wished to continue enjoying the scene but, "Breakfast is ready," was announced. We reluctantly left towards the dining hall. Hot idlis and sambar followed by filter coffee were served. It was extremely satisfying and quelled the morning appetite!

Around 11 AM, as I sat reading the morning newspaper on my cell phone the twins came again, with Alaska and Mego, their pet cats in tow. "Come Nanu, the cats need to go out. They love to play in the garden. Once they caught a butterfly too," said Nitty.

As we let the cats out, there was a cacophony of bird sounds. I thought that the birds were afraid of the cats, thus the bird chatter. Suddenly the cats jumped and climbed the neem tree. I asked Amy in surprise, "Why are the cats climbing the tree?"

Amy just shrugged looking equally surprised. The mystery was solved in a little while. Amy barely whispered, "Oh Nanu, it is Kaaliya the snake. It has crawled up the tree to feast on the fledglings of Gossipy Mynah."

As it slowly approached the tree hole, the pair of mynahs took turns to dive and peck Kaaliya. The crafty reptile would just turn its body away to avoid the sharp beaks of the bird and kept going ahead.

By now Alaska and Mego had taken positions on two branches facing the tree hole. They gave out a war cry to Kaaliya, baring their teeth. The hair on their rumps stood on end and their tails were moved slowly from side to side; they were positioned as if they were about to pounce on Kaaliya. Now, the hungry snake was on its back foot. It did give out a brave 'hiss' but it knew that his battle was lost. Hooks the parakeets also decided to have some fun and they joined the mynahs in pecking the snake. Slowly, the snake began its downwards journey. Mama Gossipy happily went inside and sat with her fledglings. The two cats also came down and scampered to Amy and Nitty, purring and rubbing against their legs.

As I was reflecting on the incident, Nitty asked, "So Nanu, what do you think, is the tree dead?"

"Well, my dear, nature always amazes me. Cats normally eat birds...but your pets actually saved the fledglings from a snake. Now coming to your question, yes, I have been seeing that despite this tree being dead, it is supporting so many lives. By removing such trees, parakeets may disappear as would so many small insects and microbes which survive on dead wood. So, we shouldn't disturb nature either by burning them or making furniture or tissue paper out of it."

Just as I thought it was time to relax, Amy foxed us with her query. "Did the cats do right in protecting the fledglings? Did Kaaliya not have a right to satisfy his hunger? Now it has to find a frog or a mouse else it will sleep hungry."

Neither did Nitty nor I have any answer. Nature follows the circle of life.

Do you have one?